For small people in big baths,
this one's for you with a big towelly hug – D.G.

For UD and AC with love xx – A.B.

BLOOMSBURY CHILDREN'S BOOKS
Bloomsbury Publishing Plc
50 Bedford Square, London, WC1B 3DP, UK

BLOOMSBURY, BLOOMSBURY CHILDREN'S BOOKS and the Diana logo are trademarks of Bloomsbury Publishing Plc

First published in Great Britain 2021 by Bloomsbury Publishing Plc

A catalogue record for this book is available from the British Library

ISBN 978 1 5266 1386 8 (HB)
ISBN 978 1 5266 1387 5 (PB)
ISBN 978 1 5266 1388 2 (eBook)

2 4 6 8 10 9 7 5 3 1

Printed and bound in China by Leo Paper Products, Heshan, Guangdong

All papers used by Bloomsbury Publishing Plc are natural, recyclable products from
wood grown in well managed forests. The manufacturing processes conform to
the environmental regulations of the country of origin.

To find out more about our authors and books visit www.bloomsbury.com and sign up for our newsletters

Little Owl's Bathtime

Debi Gliori   Alison Brown

BLOOMSBURY
CHILDREN'S BOOKS

LONDON   OXFORD   NEW YORK   NEW DELHI   SYDNEY

Little Owl was playing king of the castle with Hedge
when he heard a rustling sound.
"Did you hear that?" whispered Little Owl.

The rustling stopped.

Little Owl took a
deep breath and said,
"HALT!
Who goes there?"

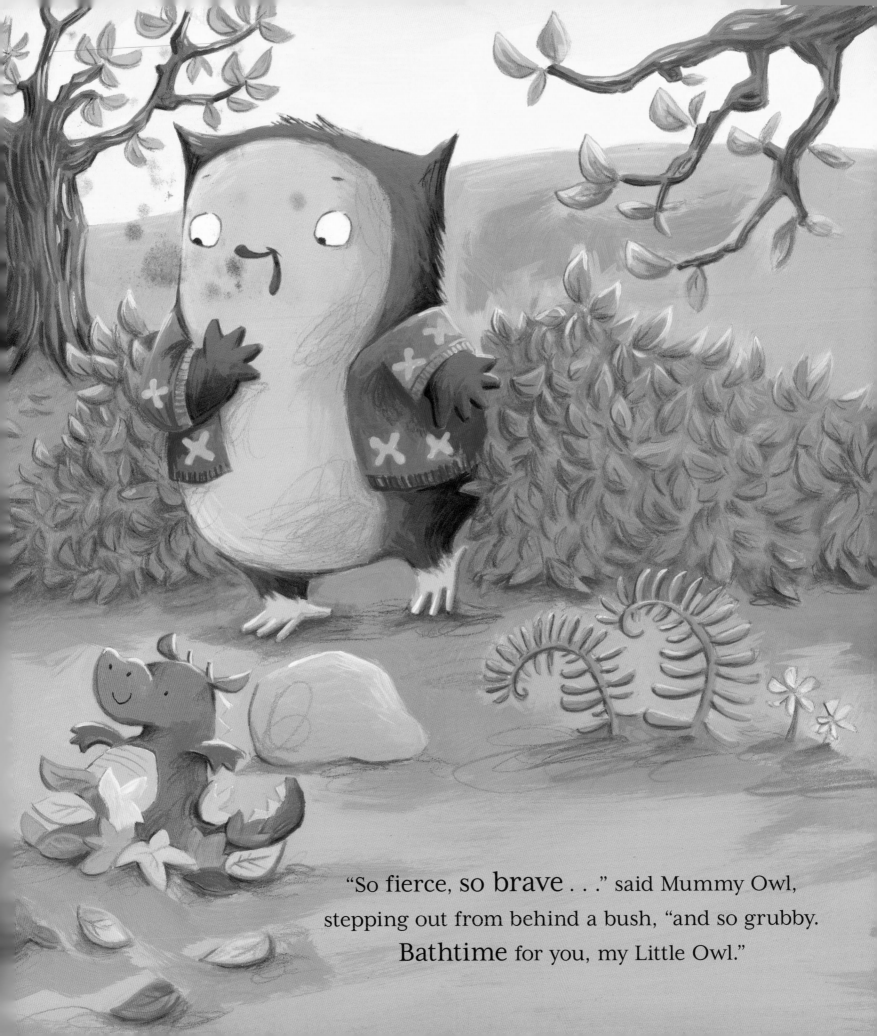

"So fierce, so brave . . ." said Mummy Owl,
stepping out from behind a bush, "and so grubby.
Bathtime for you, my Little Owl."

"NO," said Little Owl.

"NO,

NO,

NO!"

"I thought you'd say that," said Mummy Owl.

"NO," said Little Owl.
"I'm too busy just now.
King Hedge needs me
to guard her castle."

Mummy Owl blinked.
"Of course," she said. "Silly me.
Perhaps Puffle could guard the castle
while you have your bath?"

Little Owl's eyes grew wide, "Puffle?"

"Yes," said Mummy Owl.
"Dragons like Puffle make brilliant castle guards.
Puffle has teeth, claws and a flamethrower.
Nobody would dare come anywhere near
King Hedge with Puffle on guard duty."

Little Owl followed
Mummy Owl inside.

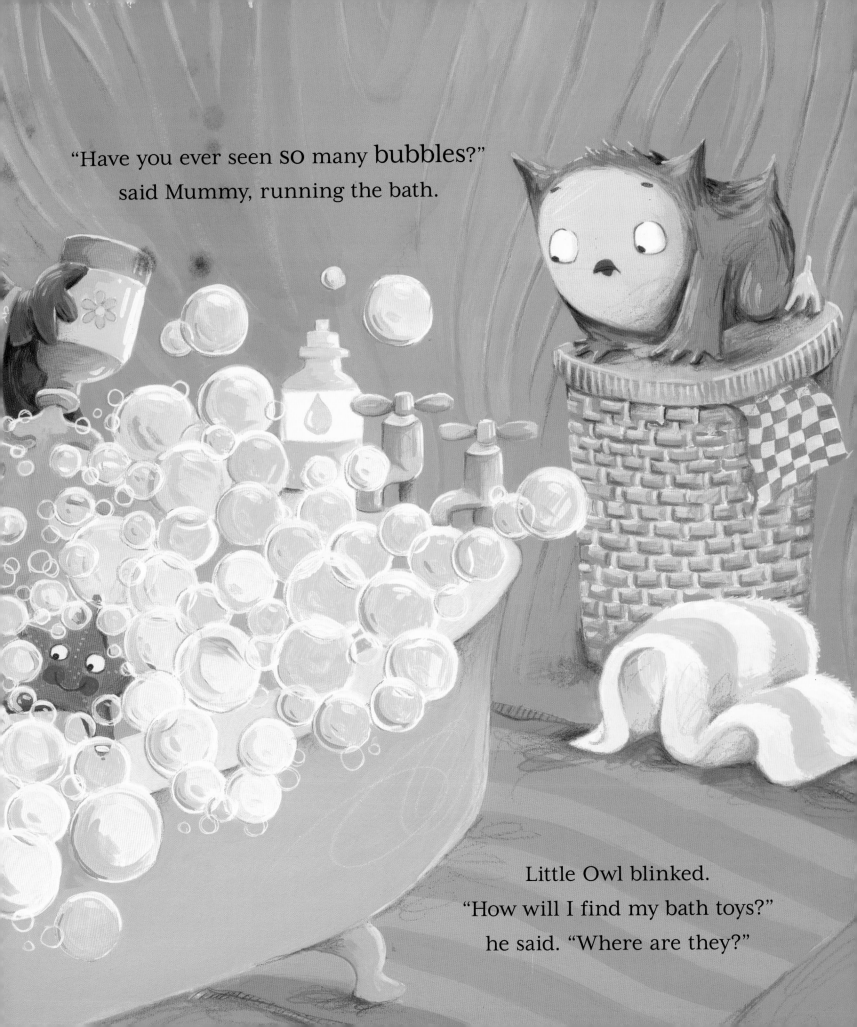

"Have you ever seen SO many bubbles?"
said Mummy, running the bath.

Little Owl blinked.
"How will I find my bath toys?"
he said. "Where are they?"

"Don't worry," said Mummy Owl.
"They're hiding in the foamy foothills of **Bubble Mountain**.
They're tricky to find but there's a marshmallow
reward if you can capture every one."

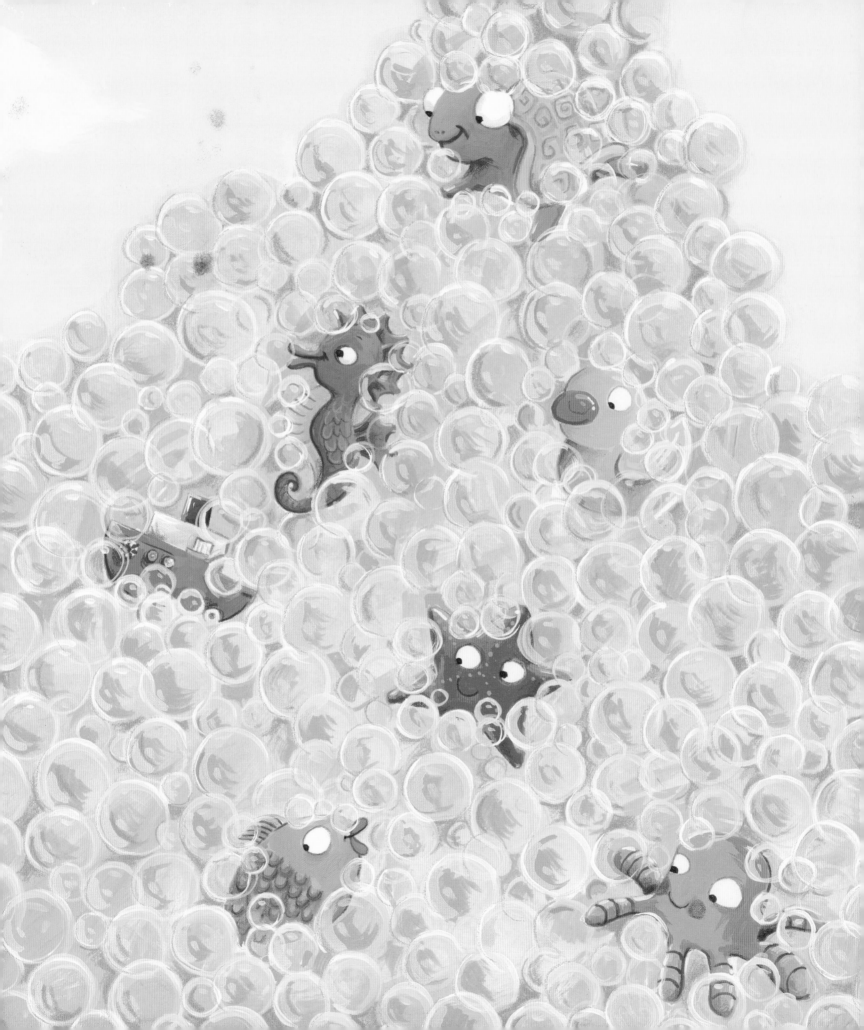

"Come on, hop in," said Mummy Owl, reaching for the shampoo.

"But, but . . . I might get soap in my **eyes**,"
said Little Owl.
"I really **wouldn't** like that!"

"Oh, Little Owl," said Mummy.
"That's not going to happen. Look . . ."

"Meet the **Towelly-Gators**," said Mummy Owl.
"These beasties like nothing better than slurping up
soapy bubbles before they can reach your eyes."

Some of the **Towelly-Gators** were big and rough,
some were **small** and **fluffy**,
but ALL of them were very **thirsty**.

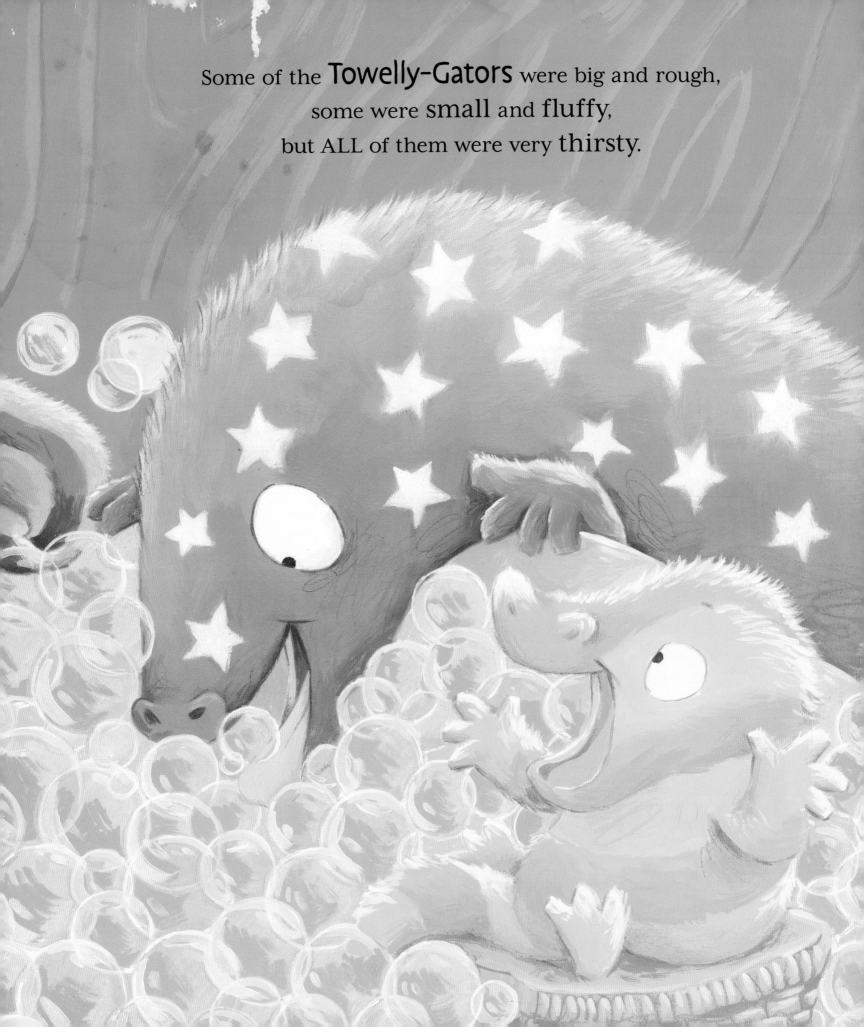

"Come on, Little Owl," sighed Mummy Owl.
"Your bath's getting cold."

"No," said Little Owl.

"Baths are boring.
I want to go back outside.

I want to play
king of the castle.

I want to finish building
my **moon rocket**.

I want to wear my
dinosaur suit.

I want . . ."

"You're right. Baths can sometimes be a bit boring,"
said Mummy Owl. "Tell you what, you go and do
all those exciting things and I'll stay here
and shampoo the **Giant Invisible Penguin**."

"A **Giant Invisible Penguin?** Here I come!" yelled Little Owl and he jumped in with a huge

KERSPLOOOSHHH!

Little Owl wallowed in the frothy foothills
of **Bubble Mountain**, captured all his hidden bath toys,
and played dive-and-seek with the **Giant Invisible Penguin**.

"Oh, Little Owl!" Mummy Owl squeaked.
"There's water **everywhere**!"

"That wasn't me," said Little Owl.
"It was the **Giant Invisible Penguin**."

"Really?" said Mummy.
"Well it's made a **giant** visible puddle. What a mess!
Time to come out and get dry in a big, warm . . ."

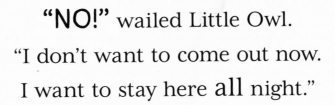

"NO!" wailed Little Owl.
"I don't want to come out now.
I want to stay here all night."

"Really?" said Mummy Owl.
"Does that mean that you and Hedge don't want
hot chocolate and marshmallows before bedtime?"

Little Owl shrieked. "HEDGE!
Hedge always sleeps in my bed."

But tonight Hedge was outside
with only Puffle to keep her safe.
What if Puffle had fallen asleep? Poor Hedge!

Little Owl leaped out of the bath,
grabbed his favourite towel and ran downstairs,
out of the door and across the garden.
"I'm on my way," he called. "Little Owl to the rescue!"

Puffle and Hedge were hiding
in a heap of soggy leaves.

"Here I am!" said Little Owl.
"Time to go home."

"Just in time for hot chocolate," said Mummy Owl.
"And marshmallows?" said Little Owl.
"Especially for you, Hedge and Puffle," said Mummy Owl.

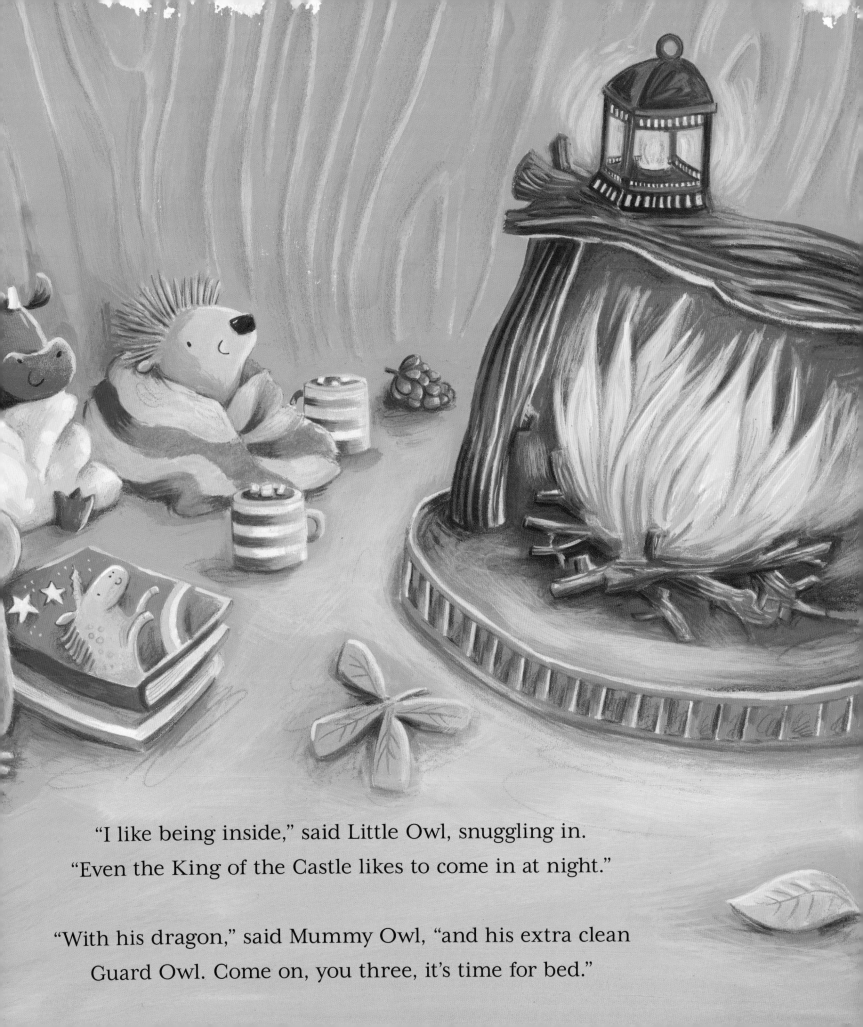

"I like being inside," said Little Owl, snuggling in.
"Even the King of the Castle likes to come in at night."

"With his dragon," said Mummy Owl, "and his extra clean
Guard Owl. Come on, you three, it's time for bed."

Little Owl peered at Hedge.
"Hedge is a bit grubby. I think she needs a bath too."

"You can give her one tomorrow,"
said Mummy, tucking Little Owl in.
"But now it's sleepy time for kings of the castle,
their dragons and guard owls.
Night, night! Sweet dreams!"

"Night, night, Mummy.
Night, night, Hedge and Puffle,"
yawned Little Owl.
"Goodnight **Towelly-gators**
and **Giant Invisible** . . ."

But Little Owl didn't manage
to say another word because
Little Owl was fast asleep.